KATIE DID!

ALSO BY KATHRYN OSEBOLD GALBRAITH

Picture Books

Spots Are Special
illustrated by Diane Dawson

For Older Readers

Come Spring

(MARGARET K. MC ELDERRY BOOKS)

KATIE DID!

by Kathryn Osebold Galbraith

ILLUSTRATED BY TED RAMSEY

A Margaret K. McElderry Book

ATHENEUM   NEW YORK   1982

LIBRARY OF CONGRESS CATALOGING IN PUBLICATION DATA

Galbraith, Kathryn Osebold.
Katie did!

"A Margaret K. McElderry book."
Summary: Mary Rose's idea of helping with the new
baby differs greatly from her mother's.
[1. Babies—Fiction.   2. Behavior—Fiction]
I. Ramsey, Ted, ill.   II. Title.
PZ7.G1303Kat   [E]   82-3981
ISBN 0-689-50237-0   AACR2

Text copyright © 1982 by Kathryn Osebold Galbraith
Illustrations copyright © 1982 by Ted Ramsey
All rights reserved
Published simultaneously in Canada by McClelland & Stewart, Ltd.
Composition by Dix Type Inc.
Syracuse, New York
Printed and bound by Halliday Lithograph Corporation
West Hanover, Massachusetts
First Edition

To Margaret "Bunny" Gabel
with affection and gratitude,
and to Elissa Lyn and Amy Elizabeth Osebold,
and once again to Steve.

"Mary Rose," Mama called. "Please stop jumping up and down, honey. I've just put the baby down for his nap."

"I'm not jumping up and down," Mary Rose said. "Katie and I are dancing for Peter."

"Well, please stop dancing then. I want Peter to go right to sleep."

"Mary Rose?" Mama called. "Please stop shouting. The baby will never go to sleep with all that noise."

"I'm not shouting," Mary Rose said. "I'm singing Peter a lullaby."

"But the baby doesn't need a lullaby right now. Please, just be a good girl and let Peter go to sleep."

"I *am* being a good girl," Mary Rose said softly. "I was just trying to help."

But Mama was too busy rocking Peter to hear.

Mary Rose tiptoed into the kitchen and poured herself a glass of orange juice. "See, I am a good girl," she told Katie. "I poured it all by myself."

Then she thought about what else she could do to help Mama.

"I know! I can put some water in Peter's bathtub. Peter loves to take a bath."

Mary Rose was very busy. When the bathtub was filled to the brim, she gave a little hop. "There! Now I'm going to make Mama and Peter a present."

It took a long time to carry everything out to the sandbox. Mary Rose began to wish there was someone to help her. It was lonely making presents all by herself.

She decided to make the presents another time. She went into the house, looking for Mama, but Mama was busy. She was in the bedroom, singing to Peter.

"Then I'll play with Tuffy," Mary Rose said.

In a little while Mary Rose heard Mama go into the kitchen.

"Mary Rose?" Mama called. Her voice was cross. "Who spilled orange juice on my clean kitchen floor? Now it's all wet and sticky."

"Ah . . . Katie did!"

"Who did?"

"Katie."

"Mary Rose?" Mama called. "Who filled Peter's tub with lilac bubble bath and green alligators?"

"Ah . . . Katie did!"

"Are you sure it was Katie?" Mama asked.

"Uh-huh. I saw her."

"Honey? Who borrowed all my pots and pans and left them in the sandbox?"

"Katie did."

"It was Katie *again?*"

"Uh-huh. She did it."

"Oh, dear," Mama said. "Who took Tuffy out of his bowl and put him in with the fishes?"

"Katie did," Mary Rose said softly.

"She put him in with the fishes? Now why did she do a thing like that?"

"Because Tuffy was lonely," Mary Rose said. "I think his mama was too busy to play with him."

"Oh," Mama said. "I see."

She took Mary Rose on her lap and held her very close. They rocked and rocked in Grandma's old rocker. Mary Rose listened to the quiet beating of Mama's heart while Mama rubbed her back.

"Katie's been very naughty today," Mary Rose said. "I think I'm going to throw her away."

"Oh, no," said Mama. "Not Katie! *I'd* never throw *you* away. I love you."

"But she made lots of messes," Mary Rose said. "And then she left the pots and pans out in the sandbox. Now they're all sandy."

"The sand will brush off," Mama said.

Mary Rose snuggled a little closer. "Katie just wanted to make sand pies for Peter and you."

"I thought so," said Mama. "And you know what?"

"What?"

"Why don't we go outside and make some sand pies together? Then we'll come in and have tea."

"Just you and me? And Katie too?" Mary Rose asked.

"Just you and me," Mama said. "And Katie too."